KU-444-205

Licensed exclusively to Top That Publishing Ltd
Tide Mill Way, Woodbridge, Suffolk, IP12 1AP, UK
www.topthatpublishing.com
Copyright © 2018 Tide Mill Media
All rights reserved
0 2 4 6 8 9 7 5 3 1
Manufactured in China

Adapted by Susie Linn
Illustrated by Jo Byatt

All rights reserved. No part of this publication may be reproduced, stored in
a retrieval system, or transmitted in any form or by any means, electronic,
mechanical, photocopying, recording or otherwise, without the prior written
permission of the publisher. Neither this book nor any part or any of the
illustrations, photographs or reproductions contained in it shall be sold or disposed
of otherwise than as a complete book, and any unauthorized sale of such part
illustration, photograph or reproduction shall be deemed to be a breach of the
publisher's copyright.

ISBN 978-1-78700-515-0

A catalogue record for this book is available from the British Library

Sing-Along
Happy Birthday to You!

Happy birthday to you,
Happy birthday to you,

Happy birthday dear JIAH,
Happy birthday to you!

Happy birthday to you,
These cards are for you,

Happy birthday dear  JIAH,
These cards are for you!

For you!

Happy birthday dear JIAH,
Birthday presents for you!

Happy birthday to you,
Decorations for you,

Happy birthday to you,
Fancy dress just for you,

Happy birthday to you,
Sparkly cupcakes for you,

Happy birthday dear JIAH,
Sparkly cupcakes for you!

Happy birthday to you,
Birthday hugs for you too,

Happy birthday!

Mind the cupcake!

Oops!

Friends are the best!

Happy birthday to you,
Party hats pink and blue,

Happy birthday dear JIAH,
Party hats pink and blue.

POP!

I'm in a tangle!

Happy birthday dear JIAH,
Party poppers, woo-HOO!

Happy birthday dear JIAH,
Let's play games just for you!

WOBBLE

Careful!

It's heavy!

Happy birthday to you,
Birthday cake made for you,

It's amazing!

Happy birthday dear JIAH,
Birthday cake made for you!

Happy birthday to you,
May your wishes come true,
Happy birthday dear JIAH,
May your wishes come true.